SCOOTER BOY

WRITTEN BY CONNIE TATE - ILLUSTRATED BY SAM BRIDGE

1

ISBN 978-1732330108

Dedicated to Cal,
who knows his way home.

Special mention to Teague,
technical advisor extraordinaire

Miles,
Always Scooter Safely!
Connie

It was about half past twelve in the afternoon,
mid-August and it was hot.
I mean really, really hot.

The sun was shining down like a
hot floodlight at Universal Studios.

I was wearing my green ninja t-shirt,
black basketball shorts,
white Converse All Star High Tops with black socks
and my LA Dodger hat,
pulled down tight with the bill in the back.

I was hot, cranky, and tired and I didn't care who knew it.

It was Friday and I wanted to shoot hoops at the beach with my bros; Milo, Lucas and Kai. But their moms picked them up hours ago.

So, instead I am waiting in the pick-up line
at Coeur D'Alene Elementary.

Not only am I standing in the pick-up line,
but I am also the only kid standing in the pick-up line,
which technically means there isn't even a line.
I'm just the last kid in the whole entire kindergarten
to still be at school, late on a Friday.

I pull my LA Dodger hat down
tighter and keep
the bill in the back
hoping no one recognizes me.

My teacher, Ms. Pippin leans over and gives me the *poor little kid whose mother can't even pick him up on time* pat on the shoulder.

I pull my LA Dodger hat down even tighter and keep the bill in the back.

Then I hear Ms. Pippin say, "Cal, Anya is here to pick you up."

Anya? I look up, keeping my LA Dodger hat pulled down tight with the bill in the back.

I twist my neck and turn my head up just enough, so I can see her, but she can't see my face.
My eyes are burning and my lips are quivering.

What is she doing here? I think it's that girl my mom said wants to be a nanny.
I don't think you wanna be a nanny dressed like that; high heel shoes, hair all twisted up and are those eyelashes? Looks like spiders crawling on her eyelids.

I mean if you wanna be my nanny you should be wearing tennis shoes to shoot some hoops before dinner and be ready to sweat.

Besides, I told my mom I don't need a nanny.

I am too big for a nanny.

I am in kindergarten.

Who needs a nanny when you are in kindergarten?

And I don't see my car.

Where is my car?

And why does she have my scooter?

And my dog! She has my dog!

I think about telling Ms. Pippin I don't know any Anya and she's probably trying to kidnap me.

But she has my scooter. . .and my dog.

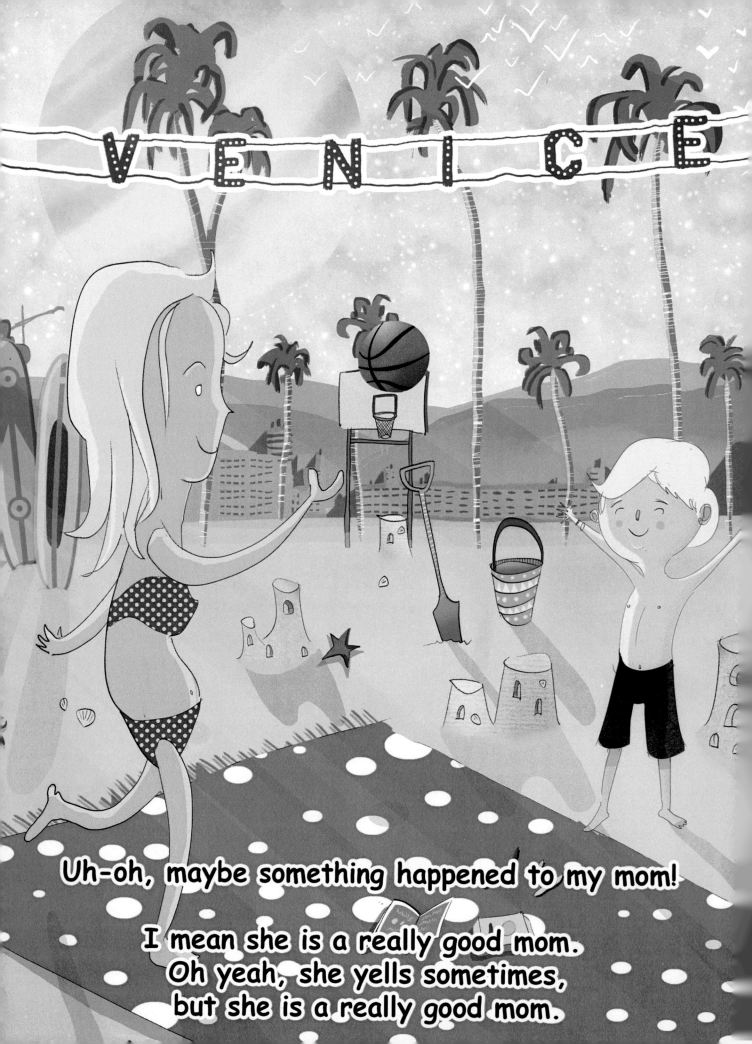

Uh-oh, maybe something happened to my mom!

I mean she is a really good mom.
Oh yeah, she yells sometimes,
but she is a really good mom.

Anya walks through the gate and
says in a *wanna be nanny* voice,

"Hi Cal. Your mom had some
errands to run after school.
She is going to meet us at your house.
Look, I have your scooter and Bo."

"Duh!" I think, but I only think it.
I don't say it out loud,
that would be rude.

But, really? I have eyes.
I can see my scooter and Bo!

Anya stops and pulls my helmet out of her giant pink purse.
Seriously? Who puts a helmet in a purse?
A professional nanny would have a backpack.

Suddenly, I know how to thwart this wanna be nanny.
My idea is so good,
I pull my LA Dodger hat down tighter
and keep the bill in the back.

I look directly at Anya and just as I am about to ask her for the secret password my mom came up with to keep me safe; you know, in case someone ever tried to talk me into going with them,
I hear Ms. Pippin.

Ms. Pippin is using her *thank goodness you're here so I can go home* **voice**.
"Hello, you must be Anya. Cal's mom called the office and they let me know you'd be picking up Cal."

I hear a sigh,
a big sigh,
a really, really big sigh,
it's me, I'm sighing.

I pull my LA Dodger hat down tighter and keep the bill in the back.

Of course, I wanted to say,
"I can get home just fine by myself!"
But instead I say, "Oh, hi Anya. Uh-okay."
I mean I don't wanna be rude
and she has my scooter and my dog.

Anya, the wanna be nanny walks toward me,
holding my helmet in one hand and stretches out her
other as if we are going to hold hands, really?
I quickly thrust my hands into my shorts.
I would have put them in my pockets,
but my shorts don't have pockets. I sigh one more time.

Then Anya, the wanna be nanny makes a mistake.
She puts my scooter on the ground and dangles
my helmet with one finger.

I pull my hands out of my shorts. Time to act.
I imagine I am on the court at basketball practice.
I don't have a basketball,
but I have two hands and fast feet.

I bounce and bob, back and forth;
I weave as if I am dribbling down the court
with the speed and agility of Steph Curry.

I grab my helmet and swing it up to my head,
pushing it down, tight over my LA Dodger hat
with the bill in the back.

With one hand I buckle the strap, tight under my chin.
With my other hand, I wave good-by to Ms. Pippin
and Anya, the wanna be nanny!

I leap onto my scooter, with my left foot on the deck;
I push off with my right. Powered by pure
kindergarten determination I spring forward, fast.
I am practically airborne as I give Bo my
here's looking at you best dog
look.

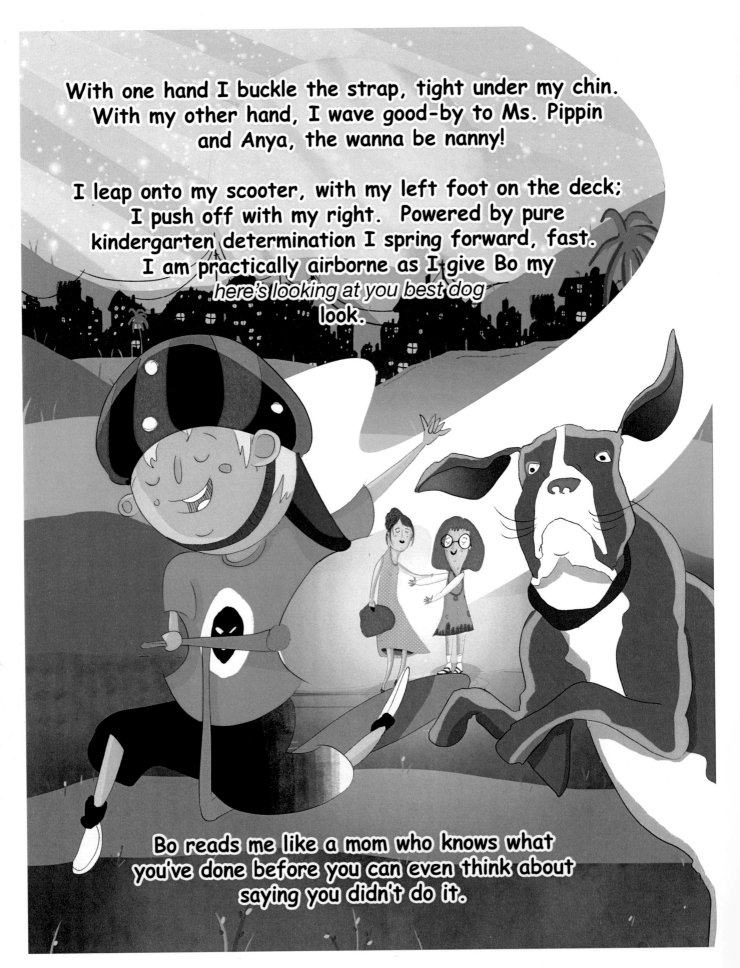

Bo reads me like a mom who knows what
you've done before you can even think about
saying you didn't do it.

Together we speed toward the crosswalk.
The crossing guard stands in the middle of
Abbott Kinney with his stop sign up holding back traffic.
It's late; this may be his last crossing.

It's now or never. Bo and I zoom through
the crosswalk and practically fly to the
opposite side of Abbott Kinney.

We did it! We are on our way home, just a boy and his dog.
We don't need a nanny. We'll show everyone!

I lean back, one foot on the deck at the back of my scooter.
The front wheel rises up and I look just like Corey Funk.
We are on the sidewalk now heading west toward
the beach, toward home.

I look quickly over my shoulder to check out the distance
between me, Bo and Anya.

Hey, what's going on?
The crossing guard is still holding up the stop sign
and Anya is crossing the street, fast, really fast!
She can really move in those high heels. She's following us!

I put my head down, my helmet strapped tightly under my chin, holding down my LA Dodger hat with the bill in the back.

Once again with my left foot on deck, I push my right foot hard against the hot, bumpy, very bumpy sidewalk.

Gotta focus, Bo and I can outrun this wanna be nanny in high heels.

Looks clear except for that rake lying across the sidewalk.

We can't slow down.

Good thing I watched that Corey Funk video.
Corey Funk says, "You have to learn how to jump,
not your ordinary jump, not a bunny jump!"

I lean back and jump forward as Bo leaps.
We are over the rake and picking up speed.

Almost to the end of Abbott Kinney,
we speed past the French café.
The city bus stop is up ahead. If we make the
green light and cross, we will leave Anya in the dust!

LE BON CAFE

We have to keep the lead. We are almost home.
I look over my shoulder again and see
Anya closing in on us, fast!

And to make matters worse Anya is yelling at an old lady
sitting at the bus stop. She is recruiting help,
the ploy of an experienced nanny. Now it is two against two!

The old woman stands, she reaches out to slow us down,
but Bo and I spring Corey Funk's third basic move into action!
I scoop my foot and kick the whip so the scooter
starts the rotation. We do a 360°!

The old lady is amazed! Actually, I am pretty amazed;
I've never done a 360° before!

Scooting along at pro-scooter speed,
we zoom past the farmers' market.
Now I know we are almost home.
I see Ms. Frieda's Fruit and Vegetable stand and
I know my house is one, two, three, only four houses away.

Another look over my shoulder to make sure we lost Anya.
Uh-oh! Anya is running fast, really, really fast!
She is running in her bare feet and closing in.

Come on Bo!
One more house and we are home!
We turn the corner and I see it,
the Suburban,
my car in the driveway with my mom behind the wheel.

Uh-oh, suddenly, my head starts throbbing under my helmet
and my LA Dodger hat with the bill in the back.
I might actually be in trouble, maybe even BIG trouble.

My mom opens the door and
I prepare for the big yell.

But, it's not a yell.
She's using her
*so glad to see my Little Pumpkin
Love Machine* **voice.**

"Anya, thanks so much for
walking Cal home.

It gave me time to pick up Cal's
buddies to shoot some hoops
at the beach.

Was he any trouble?"

Here it comes,
I am about to be ratted out
by this wanna be nanny.

I start to sweat and not because
it is mid-August and hot,
really, really hot.

Then I hear Anya say in an *I got you covered* voice,

"Not at all! We had an exciting walk home.
I can't wait to do it again."

And with that Anya smiles and gives me a fist bump.

I hear a voice, someone's talking, it's me, I'm talking.
"Hey Anya, you wanna go to the beach and shoot some hoops?"

Then I take off my helmet, climb into the Suburban
and pull my LA Dodger hat down tight
and keep the bill in the back.

Author, Connie Tate, Ed.D. has enjoyed a career in education for more than 40 years.

Her own love of reading led her to a career which specialized in promoting best practices for all readers.

Recently retired from public education she has taken up the pen to write about every day experiences through the eyes of children.

Connie resides with her husband Mick in Turlock, California.

She has three adult daughters and ten grandchildren.

Scooter Boy is her second children's book and brings her favorite quote to life:
"There are lives I can imagine without children but none of them have the same laughter and noise." - Brian Andreas

To learn more about Dr. Tate and tips for helping children develop a love for reading at:

www.rollonreading.com

Sam Bridge is an illustrator and muralist living in London and New York with his wife Ali and his cat Margarita.

He was always drawing and painting from a young age and ended up going to the school to study Fine Art.

Sam creates his work using a variety of techniques from watercolour painting, paper scribbling, spray paint, Lamy pen and knits everything together using Photoshop.

He lives by his favourite quote:
"It is simply this: do not tire, never lose interest, never grow indifferent - lose your invaluable curiosity and you let yourself die. It's as simple as that."
- Tove Jansson,

To see more of Sam's illustration work visit:

www.sambridgeart.com

Made in the USA
San Bernardino, CA
19 September 2018